© 2012 Disney Enterprises, Inc.
Published by Hachette Partworks Ltd
ISBN: 978-1-908648-32-7
Date of Printing: January 2012
Printed in Singapore by Tien Wah Press

Lady and the Tramp II

SCAMP'S ADVENTURE

Disney

Hachette

Lady and Tramp thought they were very lucky dogs. They lived with a loving family – Jim Dear, his wife Darling and their young son Junior.

Lady and Tramp had a lively family of their own. The girls – Annette, Collette and Danielle – were smaller versions of Lady. Their son's name was Scamp, and he looked just like his father.

But Scamp didn't always think he was such a lucky dog. He thought he had to follow too many rules!

Scamp always seemed
to be getting into trouble.
"Scamp!" Tramp scolded. "Don't
climb on the furniture!" And Scamp was always being
made to have a bath. "When you live in a house, you
need to be clean," Tramp reminded his son.

Scamp couldn't
even play with
Junior without
getting into trouble.
They both loved
to play tug-of-war.
But even that
usually ended in a
scolding for Scamp.

"Scamp!" yelled
Jim Dear. "I've told
you a thousand
times... NO!" Then
Jim Dear sighed
and hung his
chewed hat up with
the others.

One day, things got
even worse for Scamp.
Junior threw a ball
out of the window, and
Scamp jumped out
after it.

Then Scamp
raced back inside
with the ball,
trailing mud
all through the
house. It was
too much for Jim
Dear.
"This time
you've gone too
far!" he shouted
at Scamp.

Jim Dear
took the pup
outside and chained
him up! Jim felt guilty.
"I'm sorry, pal, but I just don't
know what else to do," he said.

Scamp was miserable. "Now, Scamp, sometimes it's hard being part of a family," said Tramp to his son. "You have to obey certain rules."

"But I want to run wild and free like a real dog!" cried Scamp.

"Son, the world out there is full of traps – and you have a family that loves you right here," said Tramp.

But Scamp still wished he could be free.

After Tramp left, a little dog about Scamp's age peeked through the fence. Her name was Angel, and Scamp thought she was the sweetest dog he had ever seen.

She smiled at Scamp.
Then she disappeared behind
the fence with some other dogs.
Poor Scamp. He wanted to follow her. He
pulled and pulled at the chain... and finally,
he broke free!

"Wait for me!"
Scamp shouted
after the mysterious
dog. He raced after
her until finally he
caught up with her.

Back at home, Lady went out to the yard with some food for Scamp. When she saw the broken chain, she knew Scamp had run away.

Lady rushed back into the house to get help.

Scamp followed Angel to a scrapyard. He couldn't believe his eyes – there were dogs running and jumping all over the place! He noticed two dogs playing tug-of-war with a hat. Another was lounging on a sofa. This was exactly the kind of life Scamp had dreamed of! He wanted to live here, with these street dogs!

Suddenly, Buster, the leader of the pack, noticed Scamp. "Nobody joins the Junkyard Dogs unless I say so," he growled. "What's your name, sport?"

"Scamp," replied the pup.

Buster wasn't sure if Scamp had what it took to be a Junkyard Dog. He decided to set Scamp a test.

When Jim Dear and Darling found out that Scamp was gone, they were very worried.

"Did you phone the dog pound?" asked Jim Dear.

"Yes, dear. They haven't got him," said Darling.

Jim Dear decided to take Lady and Tramp and search for Scamp.

Meanwhile, Buster had taken Scamp to a narrow
alley in the city. "You gotta pass a little test of
courage, in Reggie's alley," announced Buster.

Buster threw a can into the darkness. "Fetch the
can outta the alley," he challenged Scamp.

All the Junkyard Dogs watched nervously as
Scamp walked into the alley. As he crept forward he
heard a rumbling sound... and almost bumped into
a huge dog, sleeping in the shadows. Scamp realised
this must be Reggie.

As Scamp edged away, he made a noise that woke
Reggie. The giant mutt growled and began to chase
after Scamp!

As Scamp raced out of the alley, he saw that Angel was caught in the dogcatcher's net.

Quick-thinking Scamp managed to free Angel... and get Reggie trapped instead! The Junkyard Dogs were very impressed with the pup.

The pack of dogs wandered over to the park.

"Hey! You saved my life," Angel said to Scamp.
"Nobody else here would've dared to do that."

Scamp said proudly, "I'm gonna be the best
Junkyard Dog there ever was!"

Then the Junkyard Dogs told him about a dog
called Tramp – the greatest street dog ever.

Just hearing Tramp's name made Buster angry.
"He met this girl, see. Queen of the kennel-club set...
name was Lady. He left the streets for the cushy
pillow life," Buster recalled.

Scamp couldn't believe his ears. His own father had been a street dog?

Buster stared at Scamp, who was scratching behind his ear. "Hey!" he barked. "The Tramp used to scratch just like that. You ain't related, are ya?"

"No way," Scamp said. He was too afraid to tell Buster the truth.

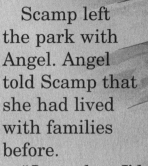

Scamp left the park with Angel. Angel told Scamp that she had lived with families before.

"Just when I'd think I'd found my forever family, they'd move, or have a new baby," she said sadly. "And I'd be back out on the street."

Angel really wanted to be in a family again. She couldn't understand why Scamp liked being on the streets. She was sure his family missed him – and she was right. Jim Dear, Lady and Tramp were searching everywhere for the pup. But by that evening, they still hadn't found any trace of Scamp.

Th
own
a big

Scamp and Angel wandered the streets together.
They came across an Italian restaurant. When the
[own]er spotted the two hungry pups, he served them
[a p]late of spaghetti and meatballs.

Scamp was falling in love with Angel. Of course, that didn't mean that Scamp was going to share his last meatball!

After their meal, Scamp and Angel walked
past Scamp's house. Just then, Jim Dear, Lady
and Tramp arrived home.

"Oh no! We gotta get outta here!" said Scamp,
pushing Angel behind a bush.

Tramp and Lady
stayed outside to talk.

"We'll find him," Lady
reassured Tramp. "You
were the best street dog
there ever was, and I
still have faith in the old
Tramp."

Angel was stunned
when she heard Tramp's
name. "The Tramp
is your father?" she
gasped. Angel couldn't
understand why Scamp
would run away from
such a loving family.

As the two of them
ran off, Scamp tried to
explain that he needed to
be wild and free.

The next day, Scamp and Angel joined the other Junkyard Dogs in the park. Scamp's family were all there too, having a picnic with Aunt Sarah and her Siamese cats. But Jim Dear and Darling were too worried about Scamp to enjoy themselves.

Aunt Sarah tried to calm them down. "Scamp will be all right," she said.

When Buster heard Aunt Sarah mention Scamp
and saw his enemy Tramp, he realised that Scamp
was Tramp's son. Buster was furious! He ordered
Scamp to take another test. If Scamp really wanted
to be a Junkyard Dog, he would have to steal a
chicken... from his own family!

Scamp agreed to the challenge.

Scamp raced down the hill and snatched the chicken. The terrified cats leapt onto Aunt Sarah, making her toss her plate of food right on Jim Dear's head!

Tramp was furious and chased after his son.

Tramp quickly caught up with Scamp.

"I'm NOT going home," Scamp declared. "It's great out here on the streets. But then, you know all about that, don't you?"

Tramp apologised for not telling Scamp that he had been a street dog. "I didn't want that life for you because I found something better. I found love," explained Tramp.

While Tramp was trying to persuade his son to come home, Buster appeared. Tramp realised that Scamp wanted to stay on the streets. He would have to learn his lesson the hard way.

"When you've had enough, our door is always open," said Tramp as he walked away.

Buster took off Scamp's collar to show he was no longer a family pet.

Scamp was thrilled. "Woo-hoo! I'm a Junkyard Dog!" he yelled. All the dogs crowded round to congratulate him.

Tramp returned to the picnic.

"He wouldn't come home," Tramp explained to Lady.

"But Tramp! He belongs with us!" Lady insisted.

"I'm afraid we're just going to have to let him figure this one out on his own. He'll come to his senses," said Tramp.

Buster led the other dogs back to the junkyard.

"How could you do that?" Angel scolded Scamp. "He's your father, go after him! You're good, decent and kind. The streets will beat that out of you if you stay," she warned.

Angel begged Scamp to leave the junkyard with her and find a nice family that they could both live with. But Scamp refused. Angel left the junkyard alone.

It wasn't long before Scamp missed Angel. Sad and lonely, he searched the streets, talking to himself. "I didn't mean it, Angel," he said. "I don't know what I was thinking."

Angel overheard him as he walked past.

Suddenly, the dogcatcher appeared and spotted Scamp.

Scamp took off like a rocket, but the dogcatcher nabbed him.

"Well lookee here. No collar. It's a one-way trip to the dog pound for you," laughed the dogcatcher.

On the way to the pound, the wagon passed Angel.

"Scamp!" Angel shouted, racing after them. But she couldn't keep up. So she rushed to Scamp's home.

"Hurry! Scamp's in trouble!" she yelled to Lady and Tramp.

Tramp rushed after Angel.

Meanwhile, there was a nasty surprise waiting for Scamp at the pound. It was Reggie!

Just as Reggie was about to attack, Tramp stormed into the pound. "Hold on, Scamp!" he shouted as he opened the latch on the cage.

Tramp quickly outwitted Reggie. Soon, father and son walked out of the pound together.

Scamp realised that the streets were too dangerous for a pup like him. So he headed back to the junkyard to get his collar back from Buster. "I'm going home – where I belong," he told Buster.

Scamp turned to his father. "I shouldn't have run away," he admitted. Then he looked at Angel. "Thanks for saving me," he said.

Back at the house, the whole family rushed outside at the sound of barking.

Junior laughed happily. "Scamp! I love you!" he cried.

Jim Dear patted Scamp's head. "It's so good to have you back where you belong!" he said.

Scamp noticed Angel at the gate, watching the happy family. He started barking.

"Jim Dear, I think Scamp brought a friend home with him," said Darling.

Jim Dear bent down. "Welcome to the family!" he said to Angel.

And from then on, it was a very, very happy family indeed – even at bathtime! the End.